I0623532

A Bit of Pickled Pumpkin

and Other Short Horror Stories

B. A. Loudon

ISBN: 978-1-9990560-4-9

A Bit of Pickled Pumpkin and Other Short Horror Stories

Edited and arranged by B. A. Loudon.

To my family and friends –

Thank you for all your endless love and unbelievable support. All of you were great sports about being beta readers for my last book, even though those stories weirded you out. Your faces and responses will forever be cherished memories.

To everyone who gave my first book a shot -

Thank you. This book is much different but I hope it's still enjoyable.

To my husband -

Thanks for letting me bounce these twisted ideas off of you and not immediately filing for divorce. I love you.

Introduction

When I was a kid, I loved scary stories. Ghost stories, or monster stories... stories that stuck with you late at night when you were supposed to be asleep.

Years later, I *still* remember some of the stories I was told on the playground in elementary, and I bet that you do too. There's just something about them that you can't quite shake, even after so long. Something that captivates your mind.

That was my goal in each of the stories here. I wanted to create a collection of stories that haunt you, haunt your thoughts, haunt your dreams. Maybe they don't scare you right away, but they linger. They creep up on you unannounced while you're doing something else, and unnerve you to your core.

Some of these stories also deal with real world problems – mental illness, domestic abuse, postpartum depression, and others. These are real world monsters, but they are not to be feared. They are to be acted on and not ignored; they can be fought and conquered.

If you or someone you know is suffering, reach out for help. Search your country's helpline numbers. There's no shame in it, and there's no reason to live in a horror.

B. A. Loudon

Promises

I've lived in this little town my whole life, unlike him. He was a man who'd seen the world. I really liked that about him. To me, it made him cultured. Exotic.

Most of the time, I was content to live in my small town. Sometimes though, listening to him talk, I'd get homesick for places I'd never been. Who knew that was even possible? Maybe he did, he always knew better and more than me after all.

He promised that he'd take me places one day. He promised that we'd see them all, together.

He promised a lot of things.

The first place he promised to take me was the Bahamas. Warm and sunny, gentle breezes, and the bluest water I'd ever seen. It sounded like Heaven to me, not that there is one, but if there were, it sounded like there.

"I promise, it's the bluest you'll ever see."

The bluest water. I used to try so hard to visualize it. It sounded so amazing. I'd shut my eyes at night and try my hardest to picture it while I waited for our promised 'someday' trip.

The bluest thing he ever showed me were the marks he'd leave on my skin.

The second place he told me he'd take me were the Lavender Fields in France. They probably smelled as beautiful as they looked. I imagined that it was the kind of smell that overtook and overwhelmed all of your senses at once.

We have a smell of that type that in our home, but I was sure that France's was more like a gentle, welcoming embrace.

The third place I'd always wanted to see were the cherry blossoms, I'm not quite sure where. Japan, I think. He's always been better with geography. He used to call me simple, and maybe I am.

Small town simple.

I just thought that they looked pretty and delicate. I dreamed of having the petals fall and dance in the air around me. Something about it just seemed so magical. I wanted magic in my life.

I guess compared to the pictures, the hand prints I left on the walls that night resembled them a bit.

I catch his eye in the mirror as I put on my lipstick. He's scared, and you know what? He should be. After our last throw-down fight, I made up my mind. No more of his empty promises. I was going to see the blue Bahama water, and the lavender fields, and the cherry blossoms. All of it, and more!

I bet he thought that burying my body under the basement floor would let him off the hook for all those stupid promises. He didn't expect me to just take *his* instead.

I smirked in the mirror.

I guess we would see everything together after all.

Just like he promised.

A Bit of Pickled Pumpkin

I know it sounds bad, but I didn't cry when she died, or at the funeral, or even at the reception. It wasn't until a few days later when I went into our pantry and saw row upon row of glass jars, all still tightly sealed, that I finally broke down.

The shelves were full of an assortment of pickled things. She loved pickles, and once she learned how easy it was to pickle things for herself, there was no stopping her. She pickled everything and anything she could get her hands on. The evidence of that was laid before me in various sized jars; eggs, asparagus, celery, apples, peaches, pork, onions, carrots... it seemed to be endless.

Our neighbour, Bill, had given her grief about it once when he saw her unloading comically large glass jars from her car. My wife being her usual self, she got him to change his tune when she showed him how easy pickling was. I think she was determined to get the whole neighbourhood into pickling. And you know what? After that little girl went missing, the neighbourhood could have used a little pickling cheer.

That's the kind of person my wife was. Happy and bubbly. When Mrs. Johnston came by to see if we'd seen her cat, my wife sent her home with a bit of pickled pumpkin and her deepest sympathies.

Strange woman, Evelyn Johnston, but sad. Grief does strange things to people. She'd lost her husband a few years earlier to a tragic accident, around the same time my wife's pickling craze started. It was a brutal mess, and they never even recovered all of him. Losing her cat must have pushed her over the edge. Derek from a few doors down said he had seen her burying a jar that looked like one of ours in her yard and talking to herself the entire time.

It would have been nice to have another person who knows what it's like to lose your significant other around to talk to, but she stepped into traffic not long after.

I was learning what grief could do. I had a pantry full of pickles – and I don't even like pickles! Or pickled anything, really. My wife tried to get me to like them, she tried so hard. Different pickled things, different additives for flavour... no combination ever seemed to work for my taste. And yet, this pickle pantry was somehow beautiful to me. Maybe I would keep it as a pickle memorial. Was that such a thing, or was it the first of its kind?

She did succeed in teaching me to pickle, bless her heart. I had to admit, the process was fun. I could see why she liked it, beyond having an endless supply of her favourite treat. There was something satisfying about the whole process, especially when the jars popped after they sealed.

That was the thing she missed the most on death row, she told me once. She wasn't able to pickle anymore.

Maybe I would continue my wife's tradition – take a jar of pickles to those in the neighbourhood needing something good. Slowly empty out the large space, one jar at a time. It would make my home a little emptier but perhaps it would make their lives a little fuller?

Pumpkin wasn't the first nor the last cat to go missing, after all.

The Performance of a Lifetime

It was her very first starring role, and she was alone on stage, about to perform the biggest monologue of the role.

She had dreamed of this moment. She should be happy. Why did she have a hollow feeling in the pit of her stomach?

Was it just nerves, or did it have something to do with the way the audience just stared at her? Their faces were blank, yet there was an air of expectation and judgment. All those eyes on her, it was enough to make anyone freeze. She couldn't though. She couldn't freeze up.

She had never performed in front of an audience of this size before, and especially not solo. Stage fright was natural, but she couldn't let it win.

No, and it wouldn't win.

She swallowed her nerves and began to speak her lines, clear and strong, just like she'd rehearsed.

Their eyes just stared at her. They seemed so empty. She tried not to notice.

When she'd gotten the call that the role was hers, she'd been elated. As third understudy, she never thought that she'd ever step foot on stage, outside of maybe a few rehearsals. She certainly hadn't expected to perform to a sold out audience! This was all she'd ever wanted – to be a stage actress, to hear the applause and cheering for her at the end, to be able to wave and bow to adoring people. Maybe even a standing ovation!

Somehow, she hadn't pictured it quite like this though. Her head swam and the lights above her were dreadfully hot. No one had warned her about how hot the lights could get.

She pressed on, her voice echoing loudly throughout the theatre.

She had a sharp pain in her neck and beads of sweat ran down her forehead – why were the lights so hot? – but like a true professional, she carried on. After all, this could be her big break; the role of a lifetime! She had to ignore her body's untimely betrayals.

Her hands trembled slightly but she hoped that no one noticed. She did her best to steady them.

The audience was still and silent. Were they judging her? Could they see how much of a mess she was beneath the façade of the character she played?

Her knees felt very weak.

Hundreds of emotionless faces, like a sea cold and devoid of feeling.

Her voice cracked and her head felt light.

The lights were so very hot!

The butterflies in her stomach refused to settle and she felt as though she might be sick.

Not now, she pleaded with herself, *please not now!*

For a second, she thought she saw something glisten offstage. Had the crew noticed her turn of health? More importantly, had the director? God, her career would be over before it even really began!

She collapsed to her knees, both because the scene called for it and because her legs could no longer hold her weight. She was grateful for the timing.

All the people.

All those faces.

Dizzy, she was so dizzy.

The stagehands rushed towards her and circled around. Wait, were they the stagehands? Her vision was suddenly blurry. They were dressed in all black so they must have been, but they were grinning and their smiles were too large and their teeth were too sharp.

She tried to stand and couldn't.

The lights...

Why were the audience still just watching? This was no longer on script! Couldn't they see that something was wrong?

The first sunk its glistening teeth into her flesh and her anguished screams filled the room.

Her voice was still clear and strong.

Then the next took its turn.

She pleaded and sobbed and wailed for help to an emotionless audience.

And the next took its turn.

Rhythmically, they took turns and they tore into her, bite after bite.

Her shrieks were both piercing and haunting, and her flesh made wet ripping noises as it was torn from her bones.

Silence.

The audience gave a roaring standing ovation.

Clean

Clean, clean, clean.

Some days, she felt as though that were all she ever did.

The stove was messy, and the counter tops had crumbs, and the appliances had fingerprints, and the floor had footprints. It was as though she'd clean it, and the mess just reappeared instantly to mock her!

It was ridiculous, but what could she do? Out came the spray bottles and the rags, and she got down to work.

Wipe, wipe, wipe.

Soon the stove was clean, the counter tops were polished, the appliances were streak-free, and the floor was immaculate.

She stood back and admired her work, basking for a moment in her sense of accomplishment.

With two children and an equally messy husband, it wouldn't stay this way for long. There was always something or rather that needed cleaning.

She sighed glumly at the thought.

Of course, there was so much else she'd rather be doing: reading a book, assembling a miniature model of something, drinking some nice tea, maybe redecorating a room.

Wouldn't that be nice indeed.

She huffed her bangs from her eyes. Best not to linger on wishful thoughts when there was still so much to do.

It was exhausting, truth be told. But no one ever asked. It was just expected. She'd clean after everyone; do all their laundry, vacuum all their carpets, wash all their dishes... It was never ending.

Never.

Ending.

As she was hanging the mop back on the wall, she heard the unmistakable sound of the back door being flung open, and mud squishing beneath the souls of children's shoes.

This was why the clean never lasted.

Her two little devils came flying through the house, covered head to toe in mud. They stopped when they saw her, and had the sense to be (or at least pretend to be) ashamed. She put her hands on her hips and tapped her toes. She pointed in the direction of the bathroom, and they dutifully marched where told.

This was her life.

It wasn't what she had wanted out of life. What had she wanted? She wasn't sure anymore. At one time she loved dinosaurs and had thought perhaps she would work in a museum, assembling the fossils. She wasn't sure what that job was called, but she assumed it would be a bit like assembling a puzzle, and she did like puzzles.

She also enjoyed decorating – maybe she'd have been an interior designer, in another life. Their home – aside from the mess – had been her canvas, and she was rather proud of it.

Unfortunately, it seemed as though no one else was.

She did so much work and it always went unnoticed.

Clean the children.

Scrub, scrub, scrub.

They fussed and protested loudly, as children do. She ignored it and continued on.

Clean the back door and all the mud down the hall.

Mop, mop, mop.

No more dirt was allowed in her house! Not a single speck! This time, it was going to stay pristine if it was the last thing she did.

Cook dinner?

Something healthy and nutritious but also quick as she had far too much to do. Throw the leftovers into a pot? The meat would be nice for a stew, and the bones would make a nice broth. Less mess that way, and less waste. Yes, that would work!

Chop, chop, chop.

Into the pot.

Plop, plop, plop.

Clean the bathroom. Again.

Bleach, bleach, bleach.

Everything needed to be white and pristine and sanitized. The bathroom and the kitchen were probably the two most judged rooms within the house, and she was not going to give anyone anything to talk about!

Clean. Clean. Clean.

When it was done, she sighed, and once more basked in a sense of accomplishment. It was clean once more.

The house was quiet. And clean! It was amazing! A miracle!

Now, what would she do?

A puzzle with the children! That would nice. A nice puzzle together, and then she'd tuck them into bed.

Her husband arrived home, late from work that night. The first thing he noticed was how quiet the house was. Their house was never quiet. Had the children gone to bed early, or was he just that late? Some days, time had no meaning.

He was relieved it was quiet, truth be told. It'd been a long day, and he wasn't sure how much more he could handle. Children bickering was the last thing he needed and would probably push him over the edge.

No one wanted Dad to snap. Mom would have to come and save the day.

He opened the door to the small bedroom as he passed by.

Two small skulls grinned back at him in the darkness – clean and white, and so very bright!

He jumped back in horror, and must have cried out.

"Is that you, dear?"

He heard his wife call to him as her footsteps grew closer. His body was numb and his mouth felt dry and useless, unable to form any words. Instead his lips just open and closed, like a fish out of water.

"Oh dear," his wife tutted, tucking the book in her hand under her arm and tapping her toes. "You're very dirty, and you've made such a mess!"

Happy White Lies

Sometimes, kids are the only ones willing to say what's really on their minds. They have no filter. They sometimes just blurt out their thoughts without reading the social cues of a room. It's part of the reason I'll never have any of my own – something I'm quite happy about!

My mom, on the other hand, was the opposite. Everything she said was through a positive, happy filter. Much of the time, there was no honesty in her cheeriness.

"Sometimes little white lies are necessary!" She had tried to explain to me once, in her overly peppy voice.

There were two problems with that statement; it was a horrible lesson for a little kid, and she would tell her 'little white lies' in situations where they absolutely were *not* necessary!

"I love this weather today!" She had said with a grin as we boarded up the windows and the tornado sirens blared throughout the town outside. The wind rattled the house as we took shelter in the bathroom, all the while she sang top us about what a beautiful day it was.

"Dinner is delicious!" She had beamed another time while we all tried our best to chew through the bits of charred meat and potatoes. She had been distracted and hadn't heard the timer on the stove go off. If it hadn't been for my brother, our house would have probably burnt down that day.

I don't know if it was the lies that bothered me so much, or the cheeriness. She was always happy. Who knew that happiness could be so infuriating? And it was downright infuriating. But the worst part was how *fake* her happiness was.

It just seemed so insane, even then to a child. She always made herself out to be so happy all the time when she clearly wasn't.

Her eyes, you see, her eyes were the giveaway. They always held how she was actually feeling.

It's weird to look back on this as an adult. I'm luckily in a good place now, and I'm happy with my life. But my childhood was strange. It's fuzzy to remember some things, but there was always this weird sense of unease, and I think it was all from my mother.

My older brother and I would sometimes exchange looks with each other when she had one of her moments, but we never said anything to her. I don't know why we didn't, but we'd just watch whatever situation play out in silence.

I did eventually say something to my mom, but it wasn't directly about the lies. "Why are you always happy?"

"Oh darling, I can't help it! It's my sunny disposition," she laughed, "it's just something I inherited from my mother! Just like you'll inherit from me!"

This confused me at the time. I wasn't always happy, so how could I inherit it? Not only that, but I realized that I didn't *want* to inherit it. I didn't want to have happy words but sad eyes.

I didn't tell her any of that, though.

Now, I can see that inheriting her 'sunny disposition' wasn't the worst thing in the world. Her annoying happiness got her – and us – through a lot of dark times.

"What about Dad?" I asked her one day. "What will I get from him?" I couldn't remember the day he left; He had been gone so long that I didn't even have any memory of him.

Her eyes darkened but she scooped me into a hug smiled as wide as she could.

"Oh my little love, you've got his inquisitive mind! He liked to ask questions too!" She brushed my hair out of my eyes and looked at me with such intensity that I'll never forget it. "He wasn't happy though, never happy enough. You must be happy like me!"

Deep in my young bones, I knew that was the truest thing my mother had ever said.

It stuck with me. It still sticks with me.

My brother witnessed this conversation, but somehow missed the gravity of it all. Or, perhaps he was just fed up and didn't care. Either way, his response was explosive.

"This is bullshit!"

"Language," my mother tutted peppily. "I love every word that comes out of your mouth, but some could be a little less colourful."

I had never heard my brother talk like this before. It might have been the first time I had even heard this 'colourful language' from anyone.

"No, Mom, this is actually bullshit," he spat back. "No one has to be happy! There's nothing to be happy about! Maybe that's why Dad left! To go be miserable like he should be allowed to do!"

"Your father is probably very happy now," Mom insisted with a smile. "Just like we are!"

"That is garbage and you know it!"

"No, I'm happy! We're all so very happy!" Her voice was strained through her teeth, but my brother was too mad to see it.

"Like hell!"

I had never heard my brother talk like this before. He was nine, but he suddenly seemed so much older. "I'm not happy!"

"*Darling.*" The word was a warning.

My brother didn't get the message.

I didn't feel very good. I had a creeping feeling deep in my stomach.

"I'M NOT HAPPY!" He repeated, but in a yell this time. "You lie! You lie and you lie and you want us to be happy all the time but that's stupid and I'm not happy!"

It happened very quickly.

I didn't get a good look at it. All I remember was that it moved very fast, faster than I've ever seen anything living move. I'm sure that in different circumstances, it would have been impressive!

I also remember that it had many limbs, like a spider, but they were more human-like. But not human. They were upside-down, or backwards perhaps. I didn't get to study it that closely, and I haven't seen it since, but I know that those limbs shouldn't have been able to move like they did.

It crawled up from our basement, up the stairs and had grabbed my brother before any of us knew what was happening.

My mother grabbed me and turned my head into her shoulder so that I couldn't see anything but the floral pattern of her shirt. She stroked my hair and whispered more lies to me.

"Everything is okay," her voice was cheery. "Everything is fine, my darling. It's such a wonderful day."

My brother screamed as it dragged him back down to the basement. He screamed and thumped as he hit every step on the way down.

He pleaded for my mother to help, but she acted as though she couldn't hear him.

"It's really beautiful today," she said as she hugged me tighter. When she pulled back and smiled at me, there were tears in her eyes.

My brother's screams and sobs lasted the rest of the night.

The silence lasted longer.

We never spoke of him again.

I never asked any questions. I couldn't. I'm not sure my mother would have had the answers either.

The rest of my childhood was uneventful. I stayed happy for my mother, and I eventually moved out once I had graduated from school. I was able to experience other emotions again, for a while. It was like letting out a breath I didn't know that I had been holding.

But I understand more now.

My mother disappeared a couple years ago. No one is sure where she went. She stopped showing up for work, and all activity on her accounts just... stopped. The police said her accounts showed 'no signs of life' but they did tell me there was a chance that she had just gone 'off the grid,' as my father had years ago.

I have no doubt that she's with my father now, and very happy.

You see, when she went missing, I inherited her sunny disposition.

I understood then the need for the little white lies.

But it's okay, don't worry about me. My life is good. Uneventful, but good. I'm single, and I've decided that I'll never have any children. But I'm happier that way! I can do anything my heart desires on my own, and that makes me happy.

Happy white lies.

The Worst Part

I couldn't believe what I was hearing. I asked her if she was joking, but her almost blank expression told me that she wasn't.

"Every last penny gone," she said. "And that's not even the worst of it," she continued, leaning across the table to get closer to me.

Her eyes gave me a hollow feeling in the very pit of my stomach. They were so composed, or maybe just resigned.

"I should have known he was crazy," her voice lamented. "You know when you see a mad scientist in the movies? That was him. I mean the wild hair, the lab coat, just everything. He was like this perfect caricature that just stepped out of a screen."

She looked tired, so tired – the type of weary that penetrates the bones and permeates the soul. I said nothing – what could I say? - and listened as she continued.

"But, he told me that he could cure her, and I was desperate. I suppose. I mean the doctors couldn't do anything, they wanted to talk about taking her off life support. We were all just waiting for her to die."

She sniffled, and I wanted to do something to console her. I didn't move. The handgun between us on the table had me frozen to my chair.

"Ever since Anthony died, losing her was my biggest fear. He never even got to meet her, how fair is that? And then they basically just rushed her straight from the womb to that box! All those wires... all the tubes..." Her voice broke. "I couldn't even touch her."

My heart ached for my friend. I knew that her life had been one tragedy after another thanks to social media, but I guess I had never really given any thought to the personal hell it had trapped her in.

"So I agreed. I paid him. What else could I do? It's not like he could have made her any worse. I'm her mother, I'm supposed to want to do all I can do for her. I'm supposed to want to help her. If this man could, then I was doing my job, right?"

I didn't answer, just listened.

"I brought him in with me to visit her one day. Told the nurses that he was her grandfather. He had this large briefcase with him."

Her hands gestured to show me how large it had been, and for the first time, I noticed that they trembled.

"As soon as we were in the room alone, he started looking over her chart. He said some things, I don't remember what. I was just so full of hope then. High on it. He suddenly announced that he could help her for sure, and he got to work pulling things out of his briefcase."

She picked up the handgun, and I held my breath. She waved it around as she spoke.

"This thing! And that thing! So many things! They all looked like medical equipment to me. Needles and vials! He started injecting things into her lines. I didn't ask what they were. Maybe he told me. I don't know."

I gulped as I waited for her to continue. Her eyes now looked so far away. "Then what?" I asked.

"That's what I was getting to. The worst part of it all."

Down the hall, a baby cried.

The baby's cry was loud and strong.

I looked at my friend with a sudden rush of joy. "She's home! She must be well now? It's a miracle!"

"No miracle, just science. That's what he said, anyways," her voice quivered, and I saw that she had tears forming in her eyes. "She's perfectly healthy, normal in every way. I brought her home three days ago. The doctors are perplexed, but here she is, healthy and fine. Average baby."

I still didn't understand.

"That's it. The worst part," she said with a bitter laugh, "is that it worked." Her laughter turned to sobbing quite suddenly.

Before I could stop her, she put the barrel in her mouth and pulled the trigger.

The Living Time Capsule

Some people in the world have too much money, and too much imagination, and not enough people to tell them 'no.'

This was the case 200 years ago with a man named Robert J. Michaels. In 2025, interest in exploring space had been renewed, and there was almost a race going between countries to see who could explore it first. I'm told the same thing happened with the race to the Moon. Everyone wanted to be the first, to claim that victory for themselves, but there were a lot of legalities and regulations that had to happen first.

Robert wasn't the only billionaire interested in making it happen, but he was the first one to just do it rather than talk about it. The history books refer to him as an eccentric but quiet man. He never talked to the media, never gave any grand speech... he just made things happen.

His grand project was announced to the world just as it was taking off to space. He had recruited 1000 people – some with technical skills, some just average civilians – paid their families handsomely, and loaded them onto a state of the art ship, and sent them blasting into space. I know, it sounds insane, but it gets crazier; these people were on a one way trip to who knows where.

He called it 'The Living Time Capsule.' The mission for this ship and its crew was to spend the rest of their lives exploring space and creating audio logs. At that time, audio was easier to transmit, or at least, the large amounts that would be collected were. At the end of 200 years, the logs would be transmitted back to Earth. Later ships would be instructed to do video logs instead.

Oh yes, it didn't stop at just the one ship. Every five years, he'd send out a new crew on a new ship. Over time, the ships grew bigger and so did the size of the crew. People worldwide actively volunteered to be on the ships. It was groundbreaking, and uniting. I suppose technically Robert was governed by Canadian law, but he built himself a base in the middle of the ocean.

I don't know all the finer details, but eventually the governments of the world decided to work with him rather than trying to stop him. Three or four ships had been sent by that time so they likely realized the futility of it. Countries held lotteries to see who would be selected to be the civilians on board the next ship. The ships grew bigger and so did the crews. Launch Day became an international holiday. Even after Robert inevitably passed away, the project continued.

As a kid, I loved it because it meant a day off of school. I grew to realize the importance of it when I realized as a teenager that the first logs from the first ships would be transmitted back to Earth within my lifetime. Why couldn't that someone be me?

I made it my mission from that day on to be the one to listen to the logs and to transcribe them. I earned degrees in linguistics, and I learned as many languages as I could. My mother will joke and say that I don't even remember what my mother tongue is. I was hungry for anything that would build my qualifications.

It paid off.

Three weeks before Launch Day, I was hired to transcribe the logs. It was a big deal, but kept very quiet. The media were alerted that someone had been chosen for the task, but my identity was kept top secret in order to protect me. I was given bodyguards. Me, bodyguards!

One week before Launch Day, the first logs came in. I was escorted from my new living quarters to my desk. Everything was high security. I was to be the only one to listen to them at first, to prevent anything from leaking to the media. I would be secluded in a soundproof room, just me and the logs. I would be transcribing by hand as a further precaution against leaks.

It was a huge honour and responsibility, and I didn't take it lightly.

I was opening The Living Time Capsule.

At first, the logs were mundane.

"We passed Jupiter today, I never realized how big it really is!"

"I made tea today. It tastes different in space. At least, I think it does."

"I hope we find aliens and I hope they're really hot. Nine hundred ninety-nine other people on this ship but there's no one I want to bang. Maybe Marshall, but only if I'm desperate."

Security watching me through the window must have wondered why I was laughing so hard when I heard that one.

If they had stayed this mundane, I wouldn't be writing this.

I started the next log, and I immediately recoiled at what I was hearing. The change was so abrupt, and it shook me. I played the next one, and it was the same.

And the next.

And the next.

I didn't want to keep listening, but I had to.

Different languages. Different voices. Men, women, even *children*. The message was the same, but the voices were different. Young and old, all repeating in unison as if they had been put on a loop.

There was terror in their voices, as though they were being forced to speak.

Something about the intensity overwhelmed my emotions. Tears streamed down my face and nausea overtook me. My stomach contents found themselves in the waste basket beside my desk.

I broke down, and sobbed like I've never sobbed before into that trash can.

That's how I stayed when two officials came in – a man and a woman, both dressed impeccably. Their faces were expressionless as they listened to the logs that had been left playing.

"We have to cancel Launch Day," I finally managed to speak.

"No," woman said flatly. "Launch Day proceeds as planned."

Had she heard what I had just heard? "But-"

"Agreed," the man spoke, and I knew he wasn't agreeing with me. "What was said on those recordings does not leave this room."

"We can't send anyone else," I tried to protest.

"We don't know if this is a one-off," the woman replied.

"500 million," I pleaded desperately, "500 *million people* are supposed to be on that ship*!*"

"This could be a one-off," the man repeated. "We won't know until the next set of logs come in. We'll reevaluate in five years time. Launch Day proceeds."

That was that.

It was also the last day I was allowed out of the compound. They decided it was smarter to imprison me to keep the contents of the logs confidential. I'm told that the happy tidbits were released to satisfy a curious public, and they were also told that the logs were still being transcribed.

Which is true, I'm still transcribing them. I have to listen to those horrid voices daily.

Even when I'm not listening to them, I can still hear them. In the shower, in bed... they never go away.

If you're reading this, I got it out somehow. I don't expect that *I'll* ever leave this compound alive, but the public needs to know the truth. Don't worry, they won't kill me just yet; I'm too qualified, you see. They'd need a team of people to replace me, and that's just a security risk that they can't afford to take.

As I write this, I can hear the sounds of the newest ship leaving Earth. Launch Day happened as usual.

A thousand voices, a thousand logs. I expect 200 years from now, whoever is doing my job will have 500 million logs to listen to.

We are not alone. Don't send anyone else.

We are not alone. Don't send anyone else.

We are not alone. Don't send anyone else!

Angel of Mercy

I didn't expect to see her here of all places. She never was one for social gatherings. It was a wonder we even met at all.

That's where I should start.

We met at a coffee shop when she was behind me in line. I felt these tiny hands on my waist before they forcefully shoved me about a foot to the right. I was about to turn around and ask what her problem was when a water droplet whizzed by my head and landed where I had been standing.

"I know it wasn't much, but no one enjoys getting dripped on first thing in the morning." Her voice was almost dreamlike and ethereal, and her presence was entrancing.

Her name was Angie. We got to talking, and she told me about her gift.

"You see the future?" I must have sounded so incredulous, and who could blame me?

"In a sense," she replied. "I can't see everything, and it's not all the time. Most times, it's not even visual. It's more intuitive. It's hard to explain."

She didn't have to explain it further to me, I had seen the proof of it earlier.

We started spending more time together. As it turned out, we had a lot in common so we became fast friends. I spent time at her place, and she spent a lot of time at mine. She was over so often that I taught her how to give me an insulin shot if I was unable to myself. It was as if we'd been friends forever.

I got to witness more of her little moments; she'd move her coffee over an inch or so on the table, made me wait five minutes before showering, she'd step over a piece of gum on the ground with extra care... it went on. Sometimes, I saw the immediate effects of her moments, but other times it would seem as though nothing happened.

"The butterfly effect," she explained. "It will be important."

I didn't understand, but I took her word for it.

It's always strange when two good friends start to drift apart. I'm not sure exactly when it started either. We went from hanging out together a couple times a week, to once a week, to once every two weeks, to maybe once a month. Texting was the same; it slowly tapered off until we only texted occasionally. It was so gradual that I really didn't notice it until it had been weeks since we'd spoken.

When she texted me to hang out, I accepted enthusiastically.

"It's nice to see that you're still alive," I teased her as she handed me a cup of hot tea.

"Sorry, life's been sort of crazy lately," Angie said as she settled into her chair. "You haven't asked me to hang out either!"

"Fair point," I sipped at my tea. "What have you been up to?"

She shrugged. "Work mostly. What about you?"

"Same old, same old. Still single, still hate my job," I laughed. "This sounds bad, but sometimes I wish my manager would just drop dead sometimes. It'd honestly make so many of our lives easier."

"Oh, that reminds me! Are you staying for dinner?"

"Yeah, sure! We ordering pizza?"

"Yeah, that sounds great. Want me to get your insulin for you?"

I was sort of impressed that she remembered when I had to take it. "Sure, thanks!"

"Usual spot?" She asked, opening my backpack.

"Yep."

"What pizza are you feeling?" She asked, finding the black case I carried everything in. "I'm thinking Hawaiian."

"I dunno, Canadian or meat lovers? We could get two mediums or something." I was half-watching her as she got it ready for me, but my mind was more focused on whether or not I wanted mushrooms on my pizza. This was my mistake.

She injected me, and almost instantly I knew that something was wrong. My lungs burned, and I soon realized that I couldn't breathe. But I couldn't struggle either. I couldn't do anything.

Angie started to sob as she curled up beside me on the couch.

"I'm sorry, I'm so sorry," she cried as she stroked my hair.

My lungs ached.

I was terrified.

I needed air.

Was this what drowning was like?

"I didn't want to do this," Angie's tears dripped onto my face. Her sorrow was genuine, though that was anything but comforting. "It's better this way. It's so much better. That semi on 14th street tonight wouldn't have stopped in time. It would have been agonizing."

I wanted to thrash, to scream, to fight, but I couldn't. I couldn't move anything.

Oh god.

I was dying.

I needed air.

I needed to breathe.

It hurt so much.

It burned.

"This is better, this is better. I'm sorry," she whispered. "It's peaceful."

It was anything but.

My last moments were full of terror, right up until it felt as though I'd fallen asleep.

It's... surreal, I guess you could say, watching someone cry over your body. Watching the paramedics work on you. Watching it be ruled as natural causes.

Which brings us back to my funeral. I guess it makes sense that she'd come; her absence would have likely been questioned by my family who knew that we were close, and no one knew the truth about what had happened in her apartment. But I was still surprised that she had the balls to show up.

But looking around at the other ghosts in the room, it would seem that I wasn't the first. It would explain why she was so calm and collected as she sat in the pew.

Her gift? Was it really better for all of us to go this way? Maybe. Maybe we would have all died gruesomely as she predicted. We don't know. But there is one thing that I know.

There is no 14th street in our town.

About The Author

B. A. Loudon is a Canadian author out of Calgary, Alberta. Her hobbies include coming up with new story ideas, obsessing over those story ideas, and then promptly abandoning those story ideas before she finishes writing them. She also enjoys making earrings.

Find her online at www.baloudonwrites.com